Howard B. Wigglebottom

and the Monkey on His Back

A Tale About Telling the Truth

Howard Binkow

Susan F. Cornelison

Howard Binkow
Reverend Ana
Illustration by Susan F. Cornelison
Book design by Tobi S. Cunningham

Thunderbolt Publishing
We Do Listen Foundation
www.wedolisten.org

This book is the result of a joint creative effort with Reverend Ana and Susan F. Cornelison.

Gratitude and appreciation are given to all those who reviewed the story prior to publication.
The book became much better by incorporating several of their suggestions.

Karen Binkow, Sandra Duckworth, Chris Fenster, Erin Gaffny, Sherry Holland, Renee Keeler, Lori Kotarba, Sarah Langner, Tracy Mastalski, Gary Norcross, Teri Poulus, Chris Primm, Laurie Sachs, Anne Shacklett, Mimi C. Savio, Karey Scholten, C.J. Shuffler, Nancey Silvers, Gayle Smith, Joan Sullivan, Carrie Sutton, Rosemary Underwood, and George Sachs Walor.

Teachers, librarians, counselors, and students at:
Alcott Elementary, Westerville, Ohio
Blackbird Elementary, Harbor Springs, Michigan
Bossier Parish Schools, Bossier City, Louisiana
Central Elementary, Beaver Falls, Pennsylvania
Chalker Elementary, Kennesaw, Georgia
Charleston Elementary, Charleston, Arkansas
Forest Avenue Elementary, Hudson, Massachusetts
Glen Alpine Elementary, Morganton, North Carolina
Golden West Elementary, Manteca, California
Interstate 35 Elementary, Truro, Iowa
Iveland Elementary School, St. Louis, Missouri
Kincaid Elementary, Marietta, Georgia
Lee Elementary, Los Alamitos, California
Meadows Elementary, Manhattan Beach, California
Prestonwood Elementary, Dallas, Texas
Sherman Oaks Elementary, Sherman Oaks, California
Walt Disney Magnet School, Chicago, Illinois
West Navarre Primary, Navarre, Florida
Washington-Franklin Elementary School, Farmington, Missouri

Printed in Malaysia by Tien Wah Press (Pte) Limited.

Second printing May 2012

ISBN 978-0-9826165-2-9

LCCN 2010933068

This book belongs to

_____

Today is show-and-tell day at school and Howard B. Wigglebottom brought his pet mouse.

"Oh cool," said Ali as she opened the cage to get a closer look and accidently let the mouse escape.

"WHO let the mouse out??"
cried Miss Bertha.

6

"The latch doesn't work very well. He gets out all the time," Howard told his teacher. He had a choice to make and telling the truth might get his good friend in trouble.

Later at recess, Howard swung the bat and hit the ball really hard. The ball flew over the fence and hit a car, smashing the headlight. "Who broke the headlight?" demanded the angry driver.

Everyone looked at Howard. He had a choice to make. He was afraid of the stranger. "I don't know who did it," he answered.

That afternoon on the bus, Nancy bragged, "My papa is a rich doctor who saves lives! What does yours do?"

Howard paused. He had a choice to make. His father had just lost his job. "Shhhh, don't tell anyone," said Howard. "My father is the Spider Bunny."

HOWARD MADE THE WRONG CHOICE.

On the way home, his brothers and sisters dared him to a race. Howard had a choice to make. He knew he would come in last. "Lately when I run my ears spin so fast I fly like a helicopter," said Howard. "It wouldn't be fair, so go ahead without me."

HOWARD MADE THE WRONG CHOICE.

Later in the day his mother asked, "Where are your shoes? Hurry! You'll be late for soccer practice." Howard didn't want to go, so he hid his shoes. He wasn't very good at soccer and didn't like all that running. He had a choice to make. "I can't find my shoes. I guess I can't go," said Howard. "Here, wear these and get ready," said his mother.

HOWARD MADE THE WRONG CHOICE.

Even though a little voice in Howard's head kept telling him that lying is wrong, it was getting easier and easier for him to do so. But he was not ready for what happened next.

Papa Wigglebottom had a favorite chair that the children called "the money chair." Sometimes coins from Papa's pocket would fall into the chair. Every Sunday, the first bunny awake would race downstairs to find the coins. The deal was that whatever was found had to be shared equally among ALL the brothers and sisters.

On Sunday morning, Howard ran downstairs before anyone else. He dug into the chair and there were TWO large, shiny fifty-cent pieces.

"These are really cool; maybe I should just keep them for myself," thought Howard as he shoved them deep into his pocket.

At breakfast Papa asked, "Did anyone find any coins in my chair this morning?" All the kids shook their heads, disappointed. Howard had a choice to make and said, "No money this week, Papa." Papa looked sadly at Howard for a long time.

HOWARD MADE THE WRONG CHOICE.

Howard had had a bad feeling about himself for a long time. He couldn't sleep that night because of all his lies, especially the one he had told his papa. He kept seeing his father's face over and over again and thinking about how sad he looked. The LIE felt like Howard had a monkey on his back.

Next morning,
Howard woke up
feeling worse. He
knew he had to
tell the truth but
he was scared it
would make his
father even sadder,
so he didn't say
anything. This
made the monkey
on his back get
bigger and bigger
and bigger.

22

At the end of the day, Howard was feeling awful about all his lying. FINALLY he listened to the little voice in his head —his conscience— that told him it was wrong to lie. He decided to tell his father the truth.

HOWARD MADE THE RIGHT CHOICE.

That night, as
soon as Papa
came through the
door, Howard told
him everything.
"I haven't been
truthful lately." And
he began to cry.

I don't have
helicopter ears.

24

25

Howard was surprised! The monkey was gone! It felt so good to finally listen to his little voice and be brave and tell the truth.

HOWARD MADE THE RIGHT CHOICE.

POOF

26

"Howard, I'm very proud of you," said Papa. "You feel much better about yourself when you tell the truth. Lying makes you unhappy and have bad feelings about yourself. No one will trust or like you if you lie to them. Let's make a list of the people you need to apologize to and ask to forgive you. Promise yourself that from now on, you will make the right choice even if you feel scared."

Howard felt good when people liked and trusted him. From that moment on, he understood that if he listened to the little voice in his head and didn't lie, the bad feeling about himself would never, ever come back. Neither would the monkey. He was very glad about that! Howard never wanted that monkey on his back again.

Howard B. Wigglebottom and the Monkey on His Back
A Tale About Telling the Truth
Suggestions for Lessons and Reflections

★HOWARD'S LIST

Howard wanted to protect his friend Ali and cover up for her. He believed it was OK to lie to help a friend, so he lied to his teacher about how the mouse got out of the cage. What do you think? Should Howard have told the teacher the truth right away or later on when no one else was listening?

Howard lied to the driver about breaking the car's headlight. The strange man looked angry and Howard felt unsafe and scared. Was it right to lie? Would it have been better to call a teacher or a grown-up right away to talk to the man? If you were Howard, what would you have done? Would you have lied too?

Why do you think Howard lied to his friend about his father being the Spider Bunny? Do you think he feared not being liked because of what his parents did or how they lived or what they looked like? How about you? Did you ever feel like lying to your friends about your family just to look good?

Howard didn't want to be last in a race so he lied about having helicopter ears. He didn't want to race just for the fun of it. Do you know anyone like that? How about you? Do you feel bad about yourself when you lose a game or a race?

Do you remember the reasons Howard lied to his mom? He didn't want to go to practice and thought his mom was going to make him go anyway, so he hid his shoes and lied about it instead of asking permission to stay home. Was it right or wrong?

Howard felt greedy about the coins he found under the chair's seat. He didn't want to share them with anyone, so he lied to his father. Did you ever do anything like that? How did you feel afterwards? Can people tell when you are lying to them? How do you feel if they call you a liar? How do you feel when people lie to you?

On page 27, his father tells him to make a list of all the people Howard needed to apologize to for not telling the truth. If you were Howard, how many people would you put on the list? How about yourself? Do you need to make a list too?

★ BEING LIKED AND ACCEPTED

Several children were asked about the people they liked the most and to explain why. They like people who share, play fair, don't make fun of others, don't tell lies, don't take things without permission, don't tell secrets and don't tell on them. In other words, children like people they can trust. We all like to have friends and want to be liked and appreciated. It's OK to have those feelings because everybody feels this way. Do you want to be liked? Help your friends trust you by always telling them the truth and being kind to them as much as you can!

★ A LITTLE VOICE INSIDE YOUR HEAD

Howard had a little voice inside his head that told him "lying is wrong." When he chose not to pay attention to the voice, he felt bad about himself and became unhappy. He felt like he had a monkey on his back, which was weird and uncomfortable.

We all have a little voice inside our head that lets us know when we are doing something wrong. Some call it our conscience, and others our "inner teacher." Pay attention and you will be able to listen to it too. When we listen to the voice and do the right thing, we feel good about ourselves and the people we care for will like and trust us. It takes bravery and practice to be able do the right thing. It's worth it though, because it's so nice to feel good!

Learn more about Howard's other adventures.

BOOKS

Howard B. Wigglebottom Learns to Listen

Howard B. Wigglebottom Listens to His Heart

Howard B. Wigglebottom Learns About Bullies

Howard B. Wigglebottom Learns About Mud and Rainbows

Howard B. Wigglebottom Learns It's OK to Back Away

Howard B. Wigglebottom Learns Too Much of a Good Thing Is Bad

Howard B. Wigglebottom and the Power of Giving: A Christmas Story

Howard B. Wigglebottom Blends in Like Chameleons: A Fable About Belonging

Howard B. Wigglebottom Learns About Sportmanship: Winning Isn't Everything

Howard B. Wigglebottom Learns About Courage

WEBSITE

Visit www.wedolisten.org

- **Enjoy free animated books, games, and songs.**
- **Print lessons and posters from the books.**
- **Email the author.**